Reddy Rattler and Easy Eagle

Reddy Rattler
and
Easy Eagle

by Mitchell Sharmat

pictures by Marc Simont

Doubleday & Company, Inc., Garden City, New York

For Marge, whose love

makes everything possible

Library of Congress Catalog Card Number 78-20924

ISBN 0-385-142 15-3 Trade
ISBN 0-385-142 16-1 Prebound
Text copyright © 1979 by Mitchell Sharmat
Illustrations copyright © 1979 by Marc Simont

Reddy Rattlesnake

was lying in the sun

on a big rock.

"I feel down,"

he thought.

"I can't coil up.

I've got no spring."

Suddenly a big shadow

covered the rock.

Reddy struck wildly

in every direction.

6

"Hold it. Hold it,"

said Easy Eagle.

"It is only me."

"You scared me,"

said Reddy.

7

"I was just checking

down on you," said Easy.

Easy landed on the rock.

"You look so awful," he said.

"What do you expect?"

hissed Reddy.

"No one likes me.

I never knew my father.

My mother left home

the day I was born."

9

"You should be more like me,"

said Easy.

"When I feel down

I flap my wings and fly

above the whole world.

Watch me."

Easy flew off.

He flew higher and higher.

He looked like a small dot

in the sky.

Then he came down

in large, slow circles.

He landed next to Reddy.

"That is all right for you,"

said Reddy.

"But I do not have wings."

"Well, flying isn't everything,"

said Easy.

"It can get lonely up in the sky."

"It is more lonely being a rattlesnake,"

hissed Reddy.

"Everybody is afraid I'll bite.

So everybody runs away."

Easy flapped his wings.

"I am here and I like you,"

he said.

"Today you do," said Reddy.

"But tomorrow you will be hungry.

Eagles eat rattlesnakes."

Reddy dove into his hole

under the rock.

"Easy Eagle doesn't eat his friends,"

said Easy.

Easy ate a berry.

"See?" he said.

"Maybe you just do not want

to eat a loser," said Reddy.

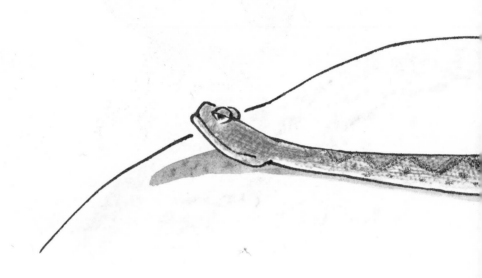

"Come out," said Easy.

"Let me scratch your back.

You will feel better."

Reddy came out.

Easy scratched his back.

"Look at me," Reddy said.

"I can't fly.

I can't run.

I can't stand tall.

I can't even sing.

All I can do is hiss."

Reddy hung down his head.

"Nobody likes a hisser.

When I hear music,

I like to sneak up and hiss

with the beat.

But when I hiss,

someone always yells,

'Here comes Bad News' . . .

and everyone leaves. FAST."

"We will have to change that,"

said Easy.

He ate a bug and thought.

"What are some good things

about you?" he asked.

"I have two good sharp fangs,"

said Reddy.

"They won't win you any friends,"

said Easy.

"What can you do?"

"I can slither and slide,"

said Reddy.

"Watch me."

Reddy slithered around the rock.

He slid down a little hill.

"That won't get you very far

very fast," said Easy.

"I can eat mice," said Reddy.

"Good," said Easy.

"There are too many mice

in the world.

Ask any farmer."

"But farmers don't like me either,"

said Reddy.

Easy picked up another bug.

"What else can you do?"

he asked.

"I can shed my skin

four or five times a year,"

said Reddy.

Easy spit out the bug

and hopped up and down.

"That's it!" he said.

"You will shed your skin

and I will trade it for mice.

Everyone will think of you as

Reddy the Skin Shedder!"

"But I don't want to be liked

just for my skin,"

said Reddy.

"I want to be liked for myself."

"Shed!" screeched Easy.

Reddy went over to a log.

He bumped and scraped against it.

Whack! Thwack! Crack!

Reddy's skin started to crack.

"It's coming!" cried Reddy.

Then Reddy wiggled and pushed
against the log.

He pulled free of his skin.

Easy grabbed the skin.

"Great!" he said.

"I will trade it.

And I will tell everyone

it comes from

Reddy the Skin Shedder."

Easy flew off.

Reddy was tired from

shedding his skin.

He fell asleep.

When he woke up

he heard Easy's wings flapping.

"Did you trade my skin?"

asked Reddy.

"Forget it," said Easy.

"I showed it to Warren Wolf.

He just laughed.

Then I tried to sell it to a man.

He pulled out a gun

and shot at me.

I was lucky to get away

with most of my feathers.

In the rush to get away

the skin fell apart."

Reddy groaned.

"I never thought

that trading skins

would make me friends.

Or keep me in mice," he said.

37

"I am not ready to give up,"

said Easy.

"Let's see.

You bite.

You bite mice most.

38

You hiss.

You slither and slide."

Easy scratched his head.

"Nothing there," he said.

"And I rattle," said Reddy.

Easy flapped his wings.

"Of course you do!

Of course you do!"

he screeched.

"What is so great about that?"

asked Reddy.

40

"Craig Coyote has a new band

at Red River," said Easy.

"He needs a rattle shaker.

You are just right for the job.

You can shake your rattles.

You can slither and slide.

You can give a soft hiss

while Craig Coyote is singing."

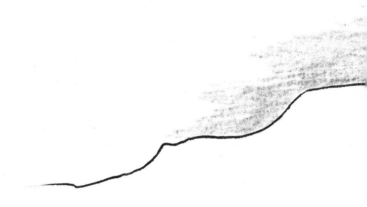

"I have never played

in a band before,"

said Reddy.

"You will be great,"

said Easy.

"I have seen you

and the other rattlers

swaying, coiling, and rattling

around a hot rock

on a warm summer night."

"You make it sound easy,"

said Reddy.

"They don't call me Easy

for nothing," said Easy.

"I will spread the news

up and down the hills

and into the desert."

"But I am Bad News,"

said Reddy.

"Remember?"

Easy hopped in a circle.

"We will give you a new name,"

he said. "How about

Reddy 'Good News' Rattler?"

"I like it! I like it!"

hissed Reddy.

"When do we start for Red River?"

"You start and I will catch up,"

said Easy.

"I have my job to do."

Reddy slithered over rocks.

He slid around bushes and trees.

He crawled up and down hills.

He slept during the heat of the day

and the cold of the night.

Easy flew across the hills.

He told everyone about

Reddy "Good News" Rattler.

Then he flew back to Reddy.

"Keep going, Reddy,"

he called.

50

"You are getting there, Reddy."

It took a week

to get to Red River.

When Craig Coyote saw Reddy,

he said,

"No rattler is good news.

He will bite the whole band.

He will keep everyone away."

Easy said, "Craig, baby,

a mouse a day

will keep the biting away.

Give the boy a chance.

He is the best rattler

in the business."

"Okay, okay,"

said Craig.

"Reddy, my boy,

show me what you can do."

Reddy raised his head.

He coiled his body

around and around.

He began to rock slowly

from side to side.

He went faster and faster.

He rattled his tail.

Whrrrrrr!

"Shake, rattle, and slide!"

cried Easy.

"Go, man, go!"

barked Craig.

Reddy was hired on the spot.

The first few days

were hard on Reddy.

He had to eat

ham sandwiches

and root beer.

Finally Craig got

a supply of mouse pies

shipped in.

Then Reddy smiled

and flicked his tongue.

He rattled as no one

had ever rattled before.

Craig Coyote's band

was a big hit.

Reddy "Good News" Rattler

was the star.

Every Saturday night

animals come to Red River.

They clap.

They dance.

They stomp their feet.

Their favorite song is

"Easy and Me."

Reddy "Good News" Rattler

wrote it himself.

If you are ever in the desert

on a Saturday night,

stop at Red River.

Give a mouse to the usher,

who is an eagle.

Then enjoy the music of Craig Coyote

and Reddy "Good News" Rattler.

But be careful.

All other rattlesnakes

are bad news!

Mitchell Sharmat has recently begun his career as a children's book writer. He is married to the well-known children's book author Marjorie Weinman Sharmat, and it was only after years of informally reading and making suggestions on her work that Mitch tried his own hand at writing. REDDY RATTLER AND EASY EAGLE is his first Doubleday book. "The move to Tucson and the opportunity to hike through the surrounding desert and mountains helped inspire the story," says Mitch. "I am fascinated by the desert and the creatures I meet there."

Mitch grew up in Massachusetts, and after graduating from Harvard he worked in retailing and real estate in New York City. He now works in financial management at his Arizona home, where he lives with Marjorie, their two sons, Craig and Andrew, and "Fritz, the world's most boring dog."

Marc Simont divides his time between a Manhattan apartment and a house in Cornwall, Connecticut. A Caldecott Award-winning artist, Marc Simont has illustrated scores of popular children's books with his wonderful pictures. Two of these books are *The Happy Day*, by Ruth Krauss, and *Nate the Great*, by Marjorie Weinman Sharmat.